FROGGY EATS OUT

FROGGY EATS OUT

by JONATHAN LONDON

illustrated by
FRANK REMKIEWICZ

SCHOLASTIC INC.
New York Toronto London Auckland Sydney
Mexico City New Delhi Hong Kong Buenos Aires

For Sean, Leah, Hannah, Emma, Stephanie, and D.J
      —J. L.

For Ed and Trudy, who also enjoy fine dining
      —F. R.

ISBN 0-439-39644-1

12 11 10 9 8 7 6 5 4 3 2 1   2 3 4 5 6 7/0

Printed in the U.S.A.   08

First Scholastic printing, September 2002

Set in Kabel

It was almost dinner time
and Froggy was hungry.
He sat in the kitchen
and dreamed about burgers
and flies.

Then he hopped up and looked for something to eat. He looked in the cabinet—*slam!* He looked in the fridge—*slam!*

He looked in the oven—*bang!* "Mom," yelled Froggy. "There's nothing good to eat!"

FRROOGGYY!

called his mother.
"Wha-a-a-at?"
"Did you forget? It's our anniversary—
we're going out to eat!"
"Hurray!" sang Froggy. "Let's go!"
"First you have to get dressed up, dear—
We're going to a *fancy* restaurant."

So Froggy flopped
to his bedroom—
flop flop flop.

He slipped off his shirt,
unzipped his pants,
took off his shoes,
pulled off his socks,
and he even changed
his underwear—
with a *zap!* of elastic.

Then he tugged on his best pants—*zip!*
buttoned up his best shirt—*zut! zut! zut!*
put on his best socks—*zoop!*
pulled on his best shoes—*zup!*
and tied them up—*zwit! zwit!*
Then he put on his best bow tie—*znap!*
and flopped out to show
his mom and dad—*flop flop flop.*

"You look very handsome, dear,"
said his mother.
"But you forgot to wash!"
"Oops!" said Froggy.

So he went to the bathroom and washed
his hands and face—*splash splash splash!*
He used lots and lots of water,
but only a little bit of soap.

Then he dried off with a towel—*zwoop!*—
and looked at himself in the mirror.
He thought he was kind of cute.

FRROOGGYY!

called his father.

"Wha-a-a-at?"

"Time to go!" said his dad.

"We'll be late!"

And off they flopped to the restaurant—
flop flop flop.

At the restaurant
Froggy's eyes grew big and round.
There were glowing candles,
flowers in vases,
and tablecloths as white as snow.

"This is a fancy restaurant," said Froggy.
"Yes," said his mother. "So remember:
Be neat,
be quiet,
and don't put your feet
on the table."

When they were seated,
Froggy said, "I'm hungry! Let's eat!"
"First we have to order, dear," said his mother.
"I want a *hamburger!*" said Froggy.
"No hamburgers here," said his father.

When the waiter handed him a menu,
Froggy opened it—
and knocked over a glass of water—*crash!*
"Oops!" cried Froggy.
"Oh, Froggy," said his mother.
"Remember what I told you?"

"I *know!*" said Froggy.
"Be neat,
be quiet,
and don't put your feet
on the table!"

But it was hard to be neat and quiet.
He fidgeted.
He shook salt on his hand
and licked it.
He banged his spoon on
the table—*bang bang bang.*

Then he hit hard on
the tip of the spoon . . .
and flipped it right into
the waiter's head—*bonk!*

After the waiter finally came
and took their orders,
they waited and waited and waited.

Froggy pulled petals off the flowers.
He blew on the candle.
He sucked on sugar cubes
and ice cubes.

Then he hopped up and flopped around
the restaurant—*flop flop flop*—singing,
"Be neat,
be quiet,
and don't put your feet
on the table!"

Froggy sat down.
Finally, dinner was served.
Froggy stuck his fork
into a huge plate of spaghetti,
and sucked some up—*sslllluuuurrrrpppp!*
It was fun, so he slurped up some more—
slurp-slurp-sssllluuuurrrrpppp!

And that's when he saw Frogilina.
She was sitting with her parents.
"Hi, Froggy!" called Frogilina.
"Who's that pretty girl frog?" asked his mother.

Froggy was so embarrassed,
he ducked beneath the tablecloth,
and pulled . . . and pulled . . .
and pulled . . .

till his spaghetti and fly sauce
landed smack on his head—*splat!*

"Oops!" cried Froggy,
looking more red in the face
than green.
"Happy anniversary!" he croaked.

"What a mess!" cried his father.
"Oh, Froggy," said his mother.
Froggy scooped spaghetti off his face,
and said, "I know—let's eat out
at a fast flies place!"
"Good idea!" said his mother.

"Let's go!" said his father.
And together they leapfrogged
all the way there—*flop flop flop* . . .

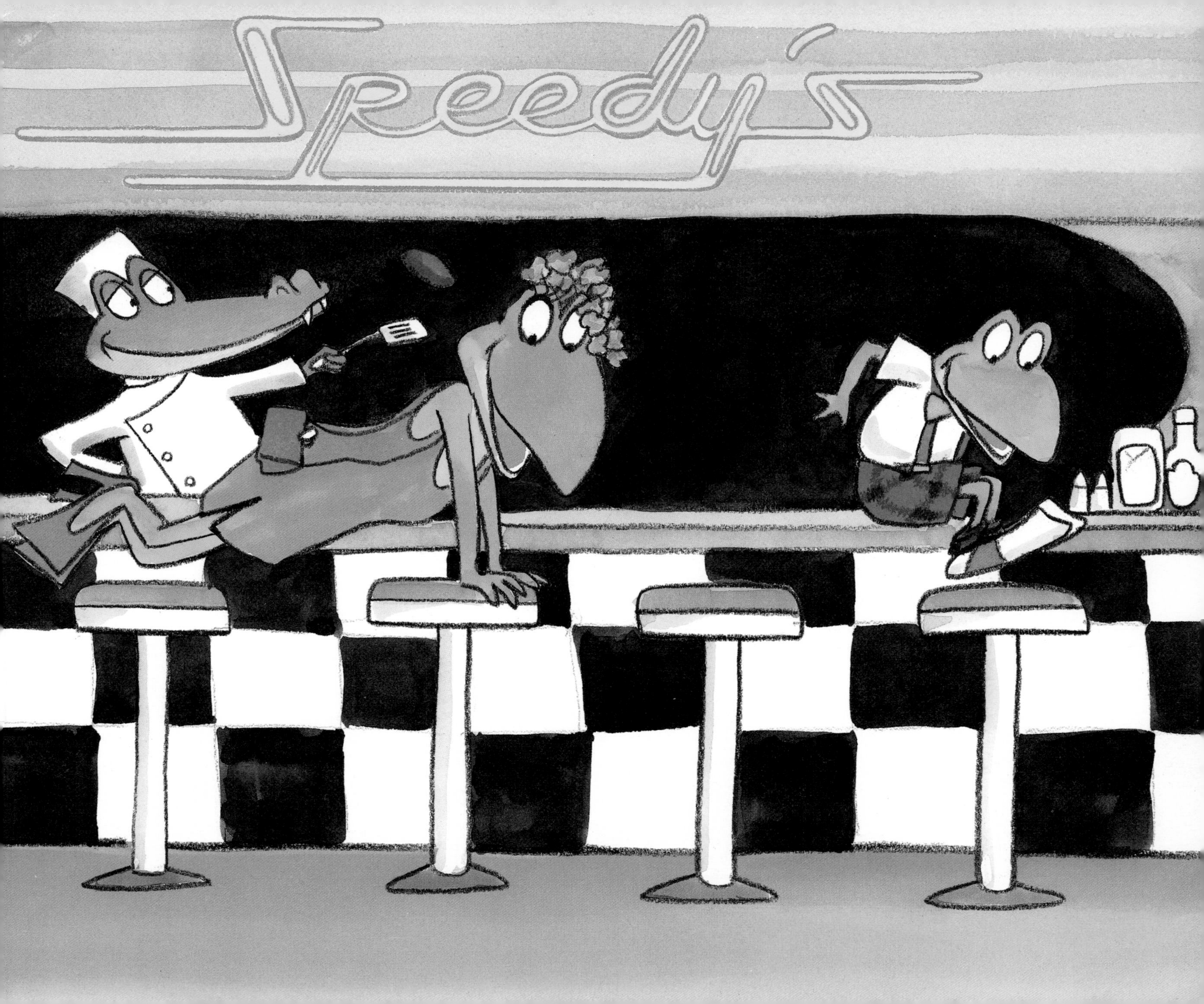
Speedy's

where they all ate burgers
and flies—*munch crunch munch.*